'Twas the Night Before Christmas

by Clement C. Moore

Adapted and illustrated by

Daniel Kirk

Abrams Books for Young Readers · New York

'Twas the night before Christmas,
when all through the house

not a creature was stirring,

except for a

mouse.

Tiny stockings were hung
by the chimney with care,
in hopes that St. Nicholas
soon would be there.

The

children

were nestled

all snug in their beds,

while visions of

yummy
treats

danced in their heads.

And Mama in her kerchief, and I in my cap,

were just settling down for a long winter's nap—

When out on the lawn
there arose such a

clatter,

I sprang from my bed
to see what was the matter.

Away to the window
I flew like a

flash,

tore open the shutters
and yanked up the sash.

The moon on the breast
of the new-fallen snow
gave a luster of midday
to objects below,

When what to my wondering eyes did appear,

but a miniature

sleigh

and eight tiny

reindeer.

With a little old driver
so lively and quick,
I knew in a moment it must be

St. Nick.

More rapid than eagles
his coursers they came,
and he whistled, and shouted,
and called them by name.

"Now, Dasher! Now, Dancer!
Now, Prancer and Vixen!
On, Comet! On, Cupid!
On, Donder and Blitzen!

"To the

top

of the porch!

To the

top

of the wall!

Now dash away! Dash away!

Dash away, all!"

As dry leaves that before the hurricane fly,

when they meet with an obstacle,

mount to the sky,

so up to the housetop

the coursers they flew,

With a sleigh full of

toys,

and St. Nicholas, too.

And then, in a

twinkling,

I heard on the roof
the prancing and pawing
of each little hoof.
As I drew in my head
and was turning around,

down the chimney
St. Nicholas came with a bound!

He was dressed like a woodsman

from his head to his foot,

and his

clothes

were all tarnished with ashes and soot.

A bundle of toys
he had flung on his back,
and I shivered with

joy

when he opened his pack.

His eyes—how they twinkled!
His dimples—how

merry!

His cheeks were like roses,
his nose like a cherry.
His droll little mouth
was drawn up like a bow,
and the beard on his chin
was as white as the snow.
He had a broad face
and a round little belly
that shook when he laughed,
like a bowlful of jelly.

He was chubby and plump,
a right jolly old elf,
and I

laughed

when I saw him, in spite of myself.

A wink of his eye
and a twist of his head
soon gave me to know
I had nothing to dread.

He
spoke
not
a word,

but quick as
a wink,

filled
all of the stockings,
then turned
with a blink.

As soon as his work
leaving presents was through,
he nodded farewell.
Up the chimney he
flew!

He sprang to his sleigh,

to his team gave a

whistle,

and away they all sped

like the down of a thistle.

But I heard him exclaim,

'ere he drove out of sight,

"Merry Christmas

to all,
and to all a good night!"

Author's Note

Clement C. Moore's poem "'Twas the Night Before Christmas"—originally entitled "A Visit from St. Nicholas"—has been with me my entire life. As a child, my father read it aloud on December evenings when the Christmas tree shimmered with tinsel, and strands of colored lights warmed the living room. As an adult, I read Moore's verse to my own three children. I collected many picture-book versions of the tale and delighted in the ways illustration can tell a story as powerfully as words.

For this, my version of "A Visit from St. Nicholas," I started with the original verse by Moore, a handwritten copy of which is housed at the New York Historical Society (www.nyhistory.org/exhibit/visit-st-nicholas). However, I chose to keep the more popular title. I also wanted to find a way to put my own touch on the classic rhyme. Since I am known for a series of books about a mouse named Sam, I thought it would be fun to tell the Christmas tale from the point of view of a mouse who just happens to be Sam's father. Though this is not a book in the Library Mouse series, the careful viewer will see how I've added details that reveal a little something about Sam's origins.

One of the curious things about "A Visit from St. Nicholas," written in the nineteenth century, is that some of the language and concepts can be a bit confusing to today's children. I know that when I read the poem to my kids, there were times I'd have to stop reading, breaking the mood to explain the phrases "settled our brains" and "just like a peddler opening his pack" or why Santa was smoking, when smoking is clearly not good for you! So while I tweaked the original to make it more of a mouse's tale, I also made some minor adjustments to update the text . . . while keeping the essential mystery and wonder that I always found in this very special poem.

For my editor and friend Howard Reeves

The images in this book began as ink drawings, with color and texture added in Photoshop.

Library of Congress Cataloging-in-Publication Data
Kirk, Daniel, author, illustrator.
'Twas the night before christmas / by Clement C. Moore ; adapted and illustrated by Daniel Kirk.
pages cm
ISBN 978-1-4197-1233-3
1. Christmas poetry. I. Moore, Clement Clarke, 1779-1863. Night before Christmas. II. Title.
PS3561.I6844T93 2015
811'.54—dc23
2014038451

Text and illustrations copyright © 2015 Daniel Kirk
Book design by Maria T. Middleton and Alyssa Nassner

Adapted from the original text of "A Visit from St. Nicholas" by Clement C. Moore, transcribed by him in 1862, a copy of which is housed at the New York Historical Society.

Printed and bound in China
10 9 8 7 6 5 4 3 2 1

Abrams Books for Young Readers are available at special discounts when purchased in quantity for premiums and promotions as well as fundraising or educational use. Special editions can also be created to specification. For details, contact specialsales@abramsbooks.com or the address below.

ABRAMS
THE ART OF BOOKS SINCE 1949
115 West 18th Street
New York, NY 10011
www.abramsbooks.com